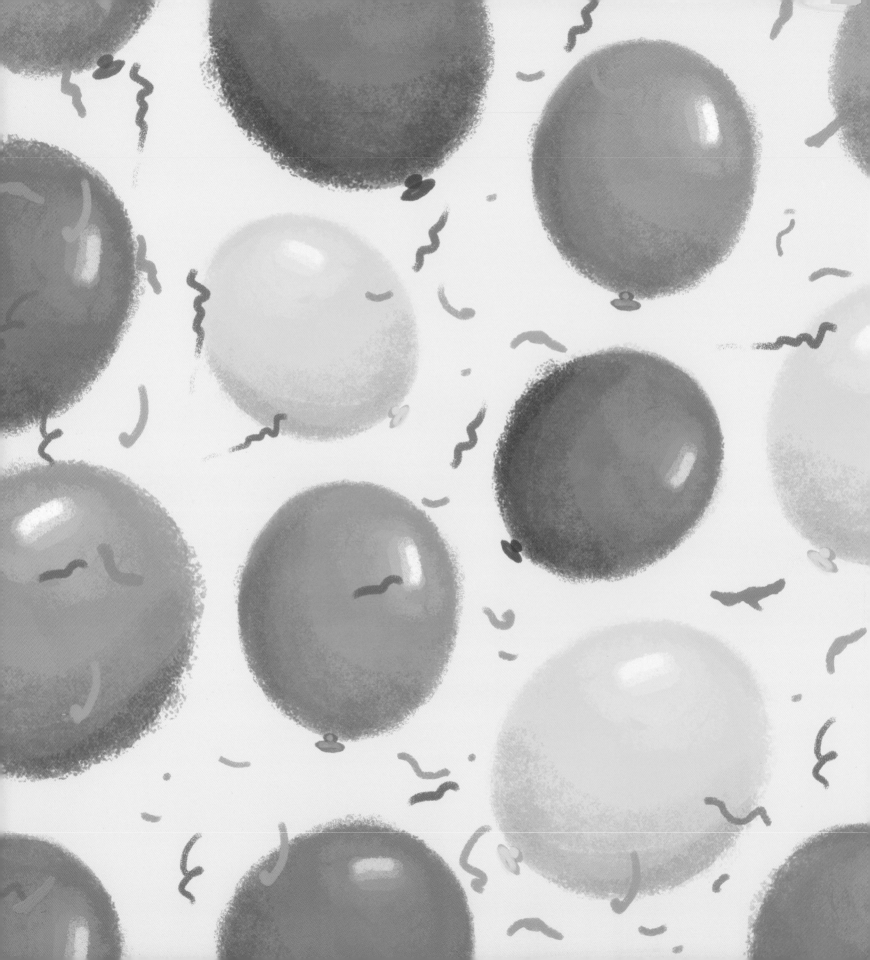

IMAGINE THAT™

Licensed exclusively to Imagine That Publishing Ltd
Tide Mill Way, Woodbridge, Suffolk, IP12 1AP, UK
www.imaginethat.com
Copyright © 2019 Imagine That Group Ltd
All rights reserved
0 2 4 6 8 9 7 5 3 1
Manufactured in China

Written by Bodhi Hunter
Illustrated by Gavin Scott

ISBN 978-1-78958-582-7

A catalogue record for this book is available from the British Library

GOOD MANNERS

Written by Bodhi Hunter

Illustrated by Gavin Scott

I say, 'Thank you!'

I say, 'Please!'

I say, 'Excuse me!'
when I sneeze!

I take my turn.

I share my toys.

Good manners are easy for girls and boys.

I say, 'Sorry.'

I say, 'Hello.'

I smile at people that I know.

I help my mum.

I help my dad.

I try to do what's good, not bad.

I have good manners. Yes, I do.
Let's see if you can do it too!

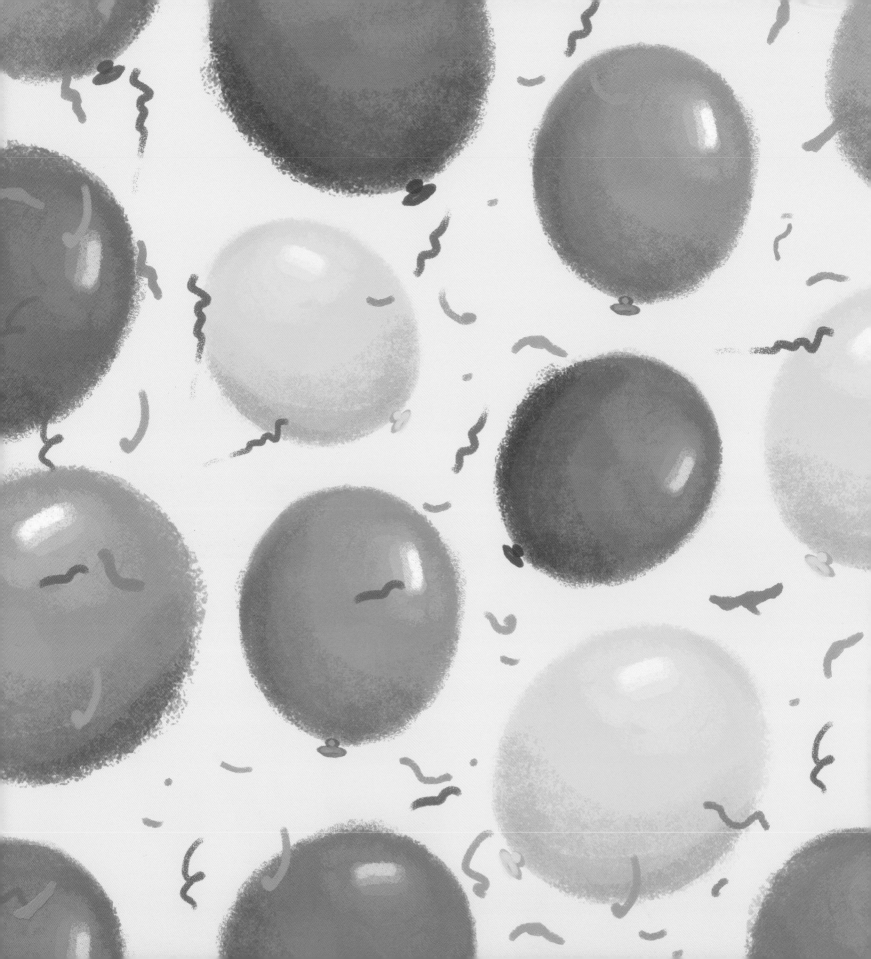

Good manners are important for little ones to learn. Join animal friends for a story about saying 'Thank you', 'Please', 'Sorry', and learning good manners.

Written by Bodhi Hunter   Illustrated by Gavin Scott

IMAGINE THAT™

Licensed exclusively to Imagine That Publishing Ltd
Tide Mill Way, Woodbridge, Suffolk, IP12 1AP, UK
www.imaginethat.com
Copyright © 2019 Imagine That Group Ltd
All rights reserved
0 2 4 6 8 9 7 5 3 1
Manufactured in China

RRP £6.99
ISBN 978-1-78958-582-7

9 781789 585827 >

IT-PCF-67-2008-179